DISCAR

DIS C A R

This book belongs to

_____

MOTHER GOOSE'S NURSERY RHYMES

MOTHER GOOSE'S NURSERY RHYMES

ILLUSTRATED BY
ALLEN ATKINSON

ARIEL BOOKS/ALFRED A. KNOPF   NEW YORK   1984

To My Godson
Taarak Prusski,
With Love

THIS IS A BORZOI BOOK
PUBLISHED BY ALFRED A. KNOPF, INC.

Library of Congress Cataloging in Publication Data

Mother Goose.
    Mother Goose's nursery rhymes.

    Summary: A collection of classic Mother Goose rhymes.
    1. Nursery rhymes. [1. Nursery rhymes] I. Atkinson,
Allen, ill. II. Title.
PZ8.3.M85   1984b   398′.8   83-48846
ISBN 0-394-53699-1

Manufactured in the United States of America
First Edition

CONTENTS

HUMPTY DUMPTY sat on a wall,
Humpty Dumpty had a great fall.
All the king's horses and all the king's men,
Couldn't put Humpty Dumpty together again.

MOTHER GOOSE'S NURSERY RHYMES

THERE WAS an old woman
Lived under a hill,
And if she isn't gone,
She lives there still.

Baked apples she sold,
And cranberry pies,
And she's the old woman
That never told lies.

AS I WAS GOING to sell my eggs,
I met a man with bandy legs,
Bandy legs and crooked toes,
I tripped up his heels, and he fell on his nose.

HICKORY, dickory, dock,
The mouse ran up the clock.
The clock struck one,
The mouse ran down,
And hickory, dickory, dock.

LITTLE TOMMY TUCKER
Sings for his supper.
What shall he eat?
Brown bread and butter.
How will he cut it,
Without e'er a knife?
And how will he be married,
Without e'er a wife?

TWEEDLEDUM AND TWEEDLEDEE
Agreed to fight a battle,
For Tweedledum said Tweedledee
Had spoiled his nice new rattle.
Just then flew by a monstrous crow,
As black as a tar-barrel,
Which frightened both the heroes so,
They quite forgot their quarrel.

DREAMS AT NIGHT are the devil's delight,
Dreams in the morning are the angels' warning.

HERE WE GO ROUND the mulberry bush,
The mulberry bush, the mulberry bush.
Here we go round the mulberry bush,
On a cold and frosty morning.

This is the way we wash our clothes,
Wash our clothes, wash our clothes.
This is the way we wash our clothes,
On a cold and frosty morning.

This is the way we clean our rooms,
Clean our rooms, clean our rooms.
This is the way we clean our rooms,
On a cold and frosty morning.

LITTLE BO-PEEP has lost her sheep,
And doesn't know where to find them.
Leave them alone, and they'll come home,
Dragging their tails behind them.

Little Bo-peep fell fast asleep,
And dreamt she heard them bleating.
But when she awoke, she found it a joke,
For they were still a-fleeting.

Then up she took her little crook,
Determined for to find them;
She found them indeed,
but it made her heart bleed,
For they'd left all
their tails behind them.

It happened one day,
as Bo-peep did stray,
Into a meadow hard by,
That she espied their tales side by side,
All hung on a tree to dry.

16

She heaved a sigh, and wiped her eye,
And over hills and dale-o,
And tried what she could, as a shepherdess should,
To tack each again to its tail-o.

SIMPLE SIMON met a pieman,
Going to the fair;
Says Simple Simon to the pieman,
Let me taste your ware.

Says the pieman to Simple Simon,
Show me first your penny.
Says Simple Simon to the pieman,
Indeed I have not any.

Simple Simon went a-fishing,
For to catch a whale;
All the water he had got
Was in his mother's pail.

Simple Simon went to look
If plums grew on a thistle;
He pricked his finger very much,
Which made poor Simon whistle.

JACK SPRAT could eat no fat,
His wife could eat no lean;
And so, betwixt them both, you see,
They licked the platter clean.

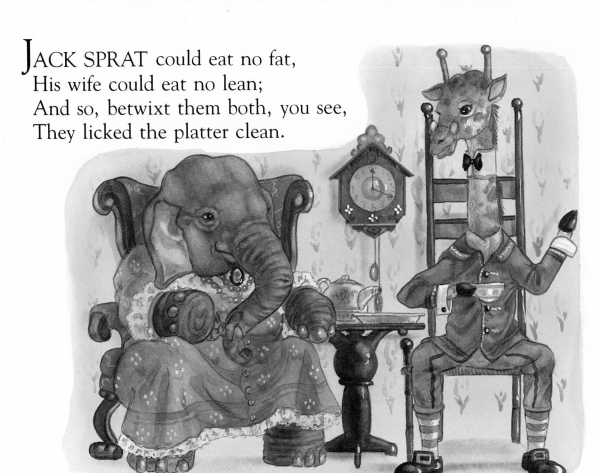

A DILLER, A DOLLAR,
A ten o'clock scholar,
What makes you come so soon?
You used to come at ten o'clock,
And now you come at noon.

19

HEY DIDDLE, DIDDLE,
The cat and the fiddle,
The cow jumped over the moon;
The little dog laughed
To see such sport
And the dish ran away
with the spoon.

Itsy bitsy spider, climbed the water spout,
Down came the rain and washed poor spider out.

Out came the sunshine,
dried up all the rain;
Itsy bitsy spider,
climbed the spout again.

One, two, buckle my shoe;
Three, four, open the door;
Five, six, pick up sticks;
Seven, eight, lay them straight;
Nine, ten, a big fat hen;
Eleven, twelve, I hope you're well;
Thirteen, fourteen, draw the curtain;
Fifteen, sixteen, maids in the kitchen;
Seventeen, eighteen, maids in waiting;
Nineteen, twenty, my stomach's empty.
Please, Ma'am, to give me some dinner.

22

THERE WAS AN OLD WOMAN TOSSED IN A BASKET
Seventeen times as high as the moon;
But where she was going no mortal could tell,
For under her arm she carried a broom.
Old woman, old woman, old woman, said I!
Whither, oh whither, oh whither so high?
To sweep the cobwebs from the sky,
And I'll be with you by and by.

OH, THE BRAVE old Duke of York,
He had ten thousand men;
He marched them up to the top of the hill,
And he marched them down again.
And when they were up, they were up,
And when they were down, they were down,
And when they were only half-way up,
They were neither up nor down.

OLD FATHER Long-Legs
Can't say his prayers;
Take him by the left leg,
And throw him down the stairs.
And when he's at the bottom,
Before he long has lain,
Take him by the right leg,
And throw him up again.

PUSSY CAT, PUSSY CAT, where have you been?
I've been to London to look at the queen.
Pussy cat, pussy cat, what did you there?
I frightened a little mouse under her chair.

As I WAS GOING to St. Ives,
I met a man with seven wives,
Each wife had seven sacks,
Each sack had seven cats,
Each cat had seven kits.
Kits, cats, sacks, and wives,
How many were going to St. Ives?

SEE-SAW, Margery Daw,
Jacky shall have a new master;
Jacky must have but a penny a day;
Because he can't work any faster.

26

SLEEP, BABY, SLEEP,
Thy father guards the sheep;
Thy mother shakes the dreamland tree,
And from it fall sweet dreams for thee.
Sleep, baby, sleep.

Sleep, baby, sleep,
Our cottage vale is deep;
The little lamb is on the green,
With woolly fleece so soft and clean.
Sleep, baby, sleep.

Sleep, baby, sleep,
Down where the woodbines creep;
Be always like the lamb so mild,
A kind and sweet and gentle child,
Sleep, baby, sleep.

THIS LITTLE PIGGY
went to market,
This little piggy stayed home;

This little piggy
had roast beef,

This little piggy had none,

And this little piggy
cried wee-wee-wee
all the way home.

THREE BLIND MICE, see how they run!
They all ran after the farmer's wife,
Who cut off their tails with a carving knife.
Did you ever see such a sight in your life,
As three blind mice?

IF I'D AS MUCH MONEY as I could spend,
I never would cry old chairs to mend,
Old chairs to mend. Old chairs to mend.
I never would cry old chairs to mend.

If I'd as much money as I could tell,
I never would cry old clothes to sell.
Old clothes to sell. Old clothes to sell.
I never would cry old clothes to sell.

LITTLE BOY BLUE, come blow your horn,
The sheep's in the meadow, the cow's in the corn.
But where is the little boy who looks after the sheep?
He's under the haystack fast asleep.
Will you wake him? No, not I,
For if I do, he's sure to cry.

FOR WANT of a nail the shoe was lost,
For want of a shoe the horse was lost,
For want of a horse the rider was lost,
For want of a rider the battle was lost,
For want of a battle the kingdom was lost,
And all for the want of a horseshoe nail.

RIDE A COCK-HORSE to Banbury Cross,
To see a fine lady upon a white horse;
Rings on her fingers and bells on her toes,
And she shall have music wherever she goes.

DING DONG BELL,
Pussy's in the well.
Who put her in?
Little Johnny Green.
Who pulled her out?
Little Tommy Stout.
What a naughty boy was that
To try to drown poor pussy cat,
Who never did any harm,
And killed the mice in his father's barn.

COCK-A-DOODLE-DOO,
My dame has lost her shoe;
My master's lost his fiddling stick,
And doesn't know what to do.

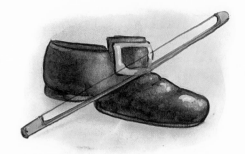

Cock-a-doodle-doo,
What is my dame to do?
Till master finds his fiddling stick,
She'll dance without her shoe.

Cock-a-doodle-doo,
My dame has found her shoe,
And master's found his fiddling stick,
Sing doodle-doodle-doo.

Cock-a-doodle-doo,
My dame will dance with you,
While master fiddles his fiddling stick,
For dame and doodle-doo.

SIX LITTLE MICE sat down to spin;
Pussy passed by and she peeped in.
What are you doing, my little men?
Weaving coats for gentlemen.
Shall I come in and cut off your threads?
No, no, Mistress Pussy, you'd bite off our heads.
Oh, no, I'll not; I'll help you to spin.
That may be so, but you can't come in.
Says Puss: You look so wondrous wise,
I like your whiskers and bright black eyes;
Your house is the nicest house I see,
I think there is room for you and for me.
The mice were so pleased
that they opened the door,
And Pussy soon had them
all dead on the floor.

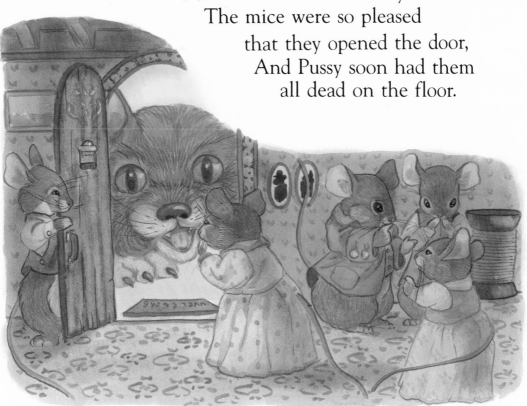

BAT, BAT,
Come under my hat,
And I'll give you a slice of bacon;
And when I bake
I'll give you a cake,
If I am not mistaken.

ONE, TWO, THREE,
four, five, six, seven,
All good children go to heaven,
Some fly east, some fly west,
Some fly over the cuckoo's nest.

DIDDLE, DIDDLE, dumpling, my son John
Went to bed with his trousers on;
One shoe off, and one shoe on,
Diddle, diddle, dumpling, my son John.

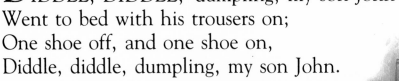

GOOSEY, goosey, gander,
Whither shall I wander?
Upstairs and downstairs
And in my lady's chamber.
There I met an old man
Who would not say his prayers.
I took him by the left leg
And threw him down the stairs.

R**ING AROUND THE ROSES,**
A pocket full of posies;
Ashes, ashes!
We all fall down.

P**ETER PIPER** picked a peck of pickled pepper
A peck of pickled pepper Peter Piper picked.
If Peter Piper picked a peck of pickled pepper,
Where's the peck of pickled pepper Peter Piper picked?

36

LONDON BRIDGE IS FALLING DOWN,
Falling down, falling down.
London bridge is falling down,
My fair lady.

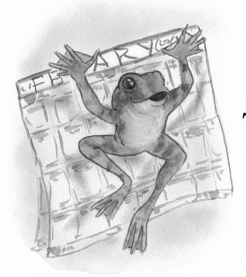

THIRTY DAYS HATH SEPTEMBER,
April, June, and November;
All the rest have thirty-one,
Excepting February alone,
And that has twenty-eight days clear
And twenty-nine in each leap year.

MARY HAD A LITTLE LAMB,
Its fleece was white as snow;
And everywhere that Mary went
The lamb was sure to go.

It followed her to school one day,
That was against the rule;
It made the children laugh and play,
To see a lamb in school.

And so the teacher turned it out,
But still it lingered near,
And waited patiently about
Till Mary did appear.

Why does the lamb love Mary so?
The eager children cry.
Why, Mary loves the lamb, you know,
The teacher did reply.

PETER, PETER, PUMPKIN EATER,
Had a wife and couldn't keep her;
He put her in a pumpkin shell,
And there he kept her very well.

Peter, Peter, pumpkin eater,
Had another, and didn't love her;
Peter learned to read and spell,
And then he loved her very well.

J ANUARY brings the snow,
Makes our feet and fingers glow.

F EBRUARY brings the rain,
Thaws the frozen lake again.

M ARCH brings breezes, loud and shrill,
To stir the dancing daffodil.

A PRIL brings the primrose sweet,
Scatters daisies at our feet.

MAY brings flocks of pretty lambs,
Skipping by their fleecy dams.

JUNE brings tulips, lilies, roses,
Fills the children's hands with posies.

HOT JULY brings cooling showers,
Apricots, and gillyflowers.

AUGUST brings the sheaves of corn,
Then the harvest home is borne.

WARM SEPTEMBER brings the fruit,
Sportsmen then begin to shoot.

FRESH OCTOBER brings the pheasant,
Then to gather nuts is pleasant.

DULL NOVEMBER brings the blast,
Then the leaves are whirling fast.

CHILL DECEMBER brings the sleet,
Blazing fire, and Christmas treat.

THIS IS THE NIGHT OF HALLOWEEN
When all the witches might be seen.
Some of them black, some of them green,
Some of them like a turkey bean.

RAINBOW IN THE MORNING,
Sailor take warning;
Rainbow at night,
Sailor's delight.

I HAD A LITTLE WIFE, the prettiest ever seen,
She washed me the dishes and kept the house clean.
She went to the mill to fetch me some flour,
She brought it home in less than an hour.
She baked my bread, she brewed my ale,
She sat by the fire and told many a fine tale.

PEASE PORRIDGE HOT,
Pease porridge cold,
Pease porridge in the pot,
Nine days old.
Some like it hot,
Some like it cold,
Some like it in the pot
Nine days old.

JENNY WREN last week was wed,
And built her nest in grandpa's shed;
Look in next week and you shall see
Two little eggs, and maybe three.

MOTHER GOOSE'S NURSERY RHYMES

TOM, TOM, THE PIPER'S SON,
Stole a pig and away did run;
The pig was eat, and Tom was beat,
And Tom ran crying down the street.

I HAD A LITTLE NUT TREE,
Nothing would it bear
But a silver nutmeg
And a golden pear.
The king of Spain's daughter
Came to visit me,
And all for the sake
Of my little nut tree.

RUB-A-DUB-DUB,
Three men in a tub,
And who do you think they be?
The butcher, the baker,
The candlestick-maker,
Turn 'em out,
knaves all three!

SOLOMON GRUNDY,
Born on a Monday,
Christened on Tuesday,
Married on Wednesday,
Took ill on Thursday,
Worse on Friday,
Died on Saturday,
Buried on Sunday.
This is the end
Of Solomon Grundy.

47

IF WISHES WERE HORSES
Beggars would ride;
If turnips were watches
I would wear one by my side.
And if "ifs" and "ands" were pots and pans,
There'd be no work for tinkers!

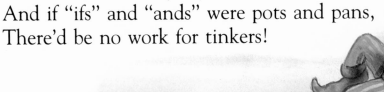

PUNCH AND JUDY,
Fought for a pie,
Punch gave Judy
A sad blow in the eye.

Says Punch to Judy,
Will you have more?
Says Judy to Punch,
My eye is sore.

GOD BLESS the master of this house,
The mistress bless also,
And all the little children
That round the table go,
And all your kin and kinsmen,
That dwell both far and near.
I wish you a merry Christmas,
And a happy New Year.

BIRDS OF A FEATHER flock together,
And so will pigs and swine;
Rats and mice will have their choice,
And so will I have mine.

OLD KING COLE
Was a merry old soul,
And a merry old soul was he;
He called for his pipe,
And he called for his bowl,
And he called for his fiddlers three.

Every fiddler, he had a fiddle,
And a very fine fiddle had he;
Twee tweedle dee, tweedle dee, went the fiddlers.
Oh, there's none so rare
As can compare
With King Cole and his fiddlers three.

PAT-A-CAKE,
pat-a-cake, baker's man,
Bake me a cake as fast as you can.
Pat it and prick it,
and mark it with a T,
Put it in the oven for Tommy and me.

IF YOU LOVE ME, love me true,
Send me a ribbon, and let it be blue.
If you hate me, let it be seen,
Send me a ribbon, a ribbon of green.

52

ROCK-A-BYE, BABY,
thy cradle is green,
Father's a nobleman,
Mother's a queen;
And Betty's a lady,
and wears a gold ring;
And Johnny's a drummer,
and drums for the king.

MARY HAD a pretty bird,
Feathers bright and yellow,
Slender legs, upon my word,
He was a pretty fellow.

The sweetest notes he always sang,
Which much delighted Mary;
And near the cage she'd ever sit,
To hear her own canary.

OLD MOTHER HUBBARD
Went to the cupboard
To fetch her poor dog a bone,
But when she got there
The cupboard was bare
And so the poor dog had none.

She went to the baker's
To buy him some bread,
But when she came back
The poor dog was dead.

She went to the undertaker's
To buy him a coffin,
But when she came back
The poor dog was laughing.

She took a clean dish
To get him some tripe,
But when she came back
He was smoking a pipe.

She went to the alehouse
To get him some beer,
But when she came back
The dog sat in a chair.

She went to the tavern
For white wine and red,
But when she came back
The dog stood on his head.

She went to the fruiterer's
To buy him some fruit,
But when she came back
He was playing the flute.

She went to the tailor's
To buy him a coat,
But when she came back
He was riding a goat.

She went to the hatter's
To buy him a hat,
But when she came back
He was feeding the cat.

She went to the barber's
To buy him a wig,
But when she came back
He was dancing a jig.

She went to the cobbler's
To buy him some shoes,
But when she came back
He was reading the news.

She went to the seamstress
To buy him some linen,
But when she came back
The dog was a-spinning.

She went to the hosier's
To buy him some hose,
But when she came back
He was dressed in his clothes.

The dame made a curtsey,
The dog made a bow,
The dame said, Your servant.
The dog said, Bow-wow.

JACK AND JILL went up the hill,
To fetch a pail of water;
Jack fell down and broke his crown,
And Jill came tumbling after.

Up Jack got, and home did trot,
As fast as he could caper,
To old Dame Dob, who patched his nob,
With vinegar and brown paper.

When Jill came in, how she did grin,
To see Jack's paper plaster;
Dame Dob, vexed, did whip her next
For laughing at Jack's disaster.

HUSH, LITTLE BABY, don't say a word,
Papa's going to buy you a mocking bird.

If the mocking bird won't sing,
Papa's going to buy you a diamond ring.

If the diamond ring turns brass,
Papa's going to buy you a looking-glass.

If the looking-glass gets broke,
Papa's going to buy you a billy-goat.

If the billy-goat runs away,
Papa's going to buy you another today.

To MARKET, to market, to buy a fat pig,
Home again, home again, jiggety-jig;
To market, to market, to buy a fat hog,
Home again, home again, jiggety-jog.

Moses SUPPOSES his toeses are roses,
But Moses supposes erroneously;
For nobody's toeses are posies of roses
As Moses supposes his toeses to be.

THE FIRST DAY OF CHRISTMAS,
My true love sent to me
A partridge in a pear tree.

The second day of Christmas,
My true love sent to me
Two turtle doves, and
A partridge in a pear tree.

The third day of Christmas,
My true love sent to me
Three French hens,
Two turtle doves, and
A partridge in a pear tree.

The fourth day of Christmas,
My true love sent to me
Four colly birds,
Three French hens,
Two turtle doves, and
A partridge in a pear tree.

MOTHER GOOSE'S NURSERY RHYMES

The fifth day of Christmas,
My true love sent to me
Five gold rings,
Four colly birds,
Three French hens,
Two turtle doves, and
A partridge in a pear tree.

The sixth day of Christmas,
My true love sent to me
Six geese a-laying,
Five gold rings,
Four colly birds,
Three French hens,
Two turtle doves, and
A partridge in a pear tree.

The seventh day of Christmas,
My true love sent to me
Seven swans a-swimming,
Six geese a-laying,
Five gold rings,
Four colly birds,
Three French hens,
Two turtle doves, and
A partridge in a pear tree.

MOTHER GOOSE'S NURSERY RHYMES

The eighth day of Christmas,
My true love sent to me
Eight maids a-milking,
Seven swans a-swimming,
Six geese a-laying,
Five gold rings,
Four colly birds,
Three French hens,
Two turtle doves, and
A partridge in a pear tree.

The ninth day of Christmas,
My true love sent to me
Nine drummers drumming,
Eight maids a-milking,
Seven swans a-swimming,
Six geese a-laying,
Five gold rings,
Four colly birds,
Three French hens,
Two turtle doves, and
A partridge in a pear tree.

MOTHER GOOSE'S NURSERY RHYMES

The tenth day of Christmas,
My true love sent to me
Ten pipers piping,
Nine drummers drumming,
Eight maids a-milking,
Seven swans a-swimming,
Six geese a-laying,
Five gold rings,
Four colly birds,
Three French hens,
Two turtle doves, and
A partridge in a pear tree.

The eleventh day of Christmas,
My true love sent to me
Eleven ladies dancing,
Ten pipers piping,
Nine drummers drumming,
Eight maids a-milking,
Seven swans a-swimming,
Six geese a-laying,
Five gold rings,
Four colly birds,
Three French hens,
Two turtle doves, and
A partridge in a pear tree.

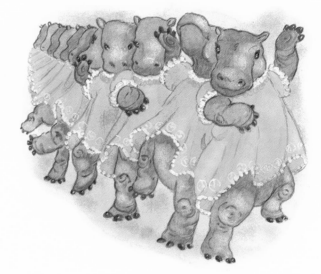

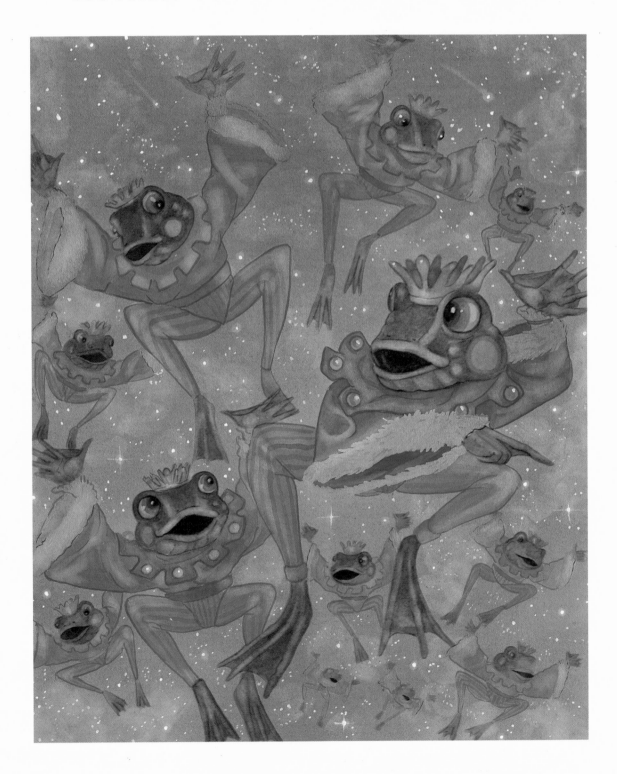

The twelfth day of Christmas,
My true love sent to me
Twelve lords a-leaping,
Eleven ladies dancing,
Ten pipers piping,
Nine drummers drumming,
Eight maids a-milking,
Seven swans a-swimming,
Six geese a-laying,
Five gold rings,
Four colly birds,
Three French hens,
Two turtle doves, and
A partridge in a pear tree.

THERE WAS AN OLD WOMAN
who lived in a shoe,
She had so many children
she didn't know what to do;
She gave them some broth
without any bread;
She whipped them all soundly
and put them to bed.

THERE WAS a crooked man,
And he walked a crooked mile,
He found a crooked sixpence
Against a crooked stile;
He bought a crooked cat,
Which caught a crooked mouse,
And they all lived together
In a little crooked house.

AN APPLE A DAY
Keeps the doctor away.
Apple in the morning,
Doctor's warning.
Roast apple at night,
Starves the doctor outright.

THREE WISE MEN of Gotham,
They went to sea in a bowl.
And if the bowl had been stronger,
My song had been longer.

LADYBUG, ladybug,
Fly away home,
Your house is on fire,
Your children will burn.

HIGGLEDY, PIGGLEDY, my black hen,
She lays eggs for gentlemen;
Gentlemen come every day
To see what my black hen doth lay.
Sometimes nine and sometimes ten,
Higgledy, piggledy, my black hen.

THE QUEEN OF HEARTS
She made some tarts,
All on a summer's day.
The Knave of Hearts
He stole the tarts,
And took them clean away.
The King of Hearts
Called for the tarts,
And beat the Knave full sore.
The Knave of Hearts
Brought back the tarts,
And vowed he'd steal no more.

STAR LIGHT, STAR BRIGHT,
First star I see tonight,
I wish I may, I wish I might,
Have the wish I wish tonight.

ROSES ARE RED, violets are blue,
Honey is sweet, and so are you.
Thou art my love and I am thine;
I drew thee to my Valentine.
The lot was cast and then I drew,
And fortune said it should be you.

70

THE LION AND THE UNICORN
Were fighting for the crown;
The lion beat the unicorn,
All about the town.

Some gave them white bread,
And some gave them brown,
Some gave them plum cake
And drummed them
out of town.

RAIN, RAIN, go away,
Come again another day.

THIS IS THE HOUSE that Jack built.

This is the malt
That lay in the house that Jack built.

This is the rat,
That ate the malt
That lay in the house
that Jack built.

This is the cat,
That killed the rat,
That ate the malt
That lay in the house that Jack built.

This is the dog,
That worried the cat,
That killed the rat,
That ate the malt
That lay in the house that Jack built.

72

MOTHER GOOSE'S NURSERY RHYMES

This is the cow with the crumpled horn,
That tossed the dog,
That worried the cat,
That killed the rat,
That ate the malt
That lay in the house that Jack built.

This is the maiden all forlorn,
That milked the cow with the crumpled horn,
That tossed the dog,
That worried the cat,
That killed the rat,
That ate the malt
That lay in the house that Jack built.

This is the man all tattered and torn,
That kissed the maiden all forlorn,
That milked the cow with the crumpled horn,
That tossed the dog,
That worried the cat,
That killed the rat,
That ate the malt
That lay in the house that Jack built.

73

MOTHER GOOSE'S NURSERY RHYMES

This is the priest all shaven and shorn,
That married the man all tattered and torn,
That kissed the maiden all forlorn,
That milked the cow with the crumpled horn,
That tossed the dog,
That worried the cat,
That killed the rat,
That ate the malt
That lay in the house that Jack built.

This is the cock that crowed in the morn,
That waked the priest all shaven and shorn,
That married the man all tattered and torn,
That kissed the maiden all forlorn,
That milked the cow with the crumpled horn,
That tossed the dog,
That worried the cat,
That killed the rat,
That ate the malt,
That lay in the house that Jack built.

MOTHER GOOSE'S NURSERY RHYMES

This is the farmer sowing his corn,
That kept the cock that crowed in the morn,
That waked the priest all shaven and shorn,
That married the man all tattered and torn,
That kissed the maiden all forlorn,
That milked the cow with the crumpled horn,
That tossed the dog,
That worried the cat,
That killed the rat,
That ate the malt
That lay in the house
that Jack built.

GOLDEN SLUMBERS kiss your eyes,
Smiles awake you when you rise.
Sleep pretty darling, do not cry,
And I will sing you a lullaby:
Rock them, rock them, lullaby.

Care is heavy, therefore sleep you;
You are care, and care must keep you.
Sleep, pretty darling, do not cry,
And I will sing you a lullaby:
Rock them, rock them, lullaby.

SING A SONG OF SIXPENCE,
A pocket full of rye,
Four and twenty blackbirds
Baked in a pie.

When the pie was opened,
The birds began to sing;
Was not that a dainty dish,
To set before the king?

The king was in his counting-house,
Counting out his money;
The queen was in the parlor,
Eating bread and honey,

The maid was in the garden,
Hanging out the clothes,
When along came a blackbird,
And snapped off her nose.
Along came a Jenny Wren
And popped it on again.

77

TWINKLE, TWINKLE, little star
How I wonder what you are!
Up above the world so high,
Like a diamond in the sky.

SOMETHING OLD, something new,
Something borrowed, something blue,
And a penny in her shoe.

HUSH-A-BYE BABY
On the tree top,
When the wind blows
The cradle will rock;
When the bough breaks
The cradle will fall;
Down will come baby,
Cradle and all.

NOW I LAY ME down to sleep,
I pray the Lord my soul to keep;
And if I die before I wake,
I pray the Lord my soul to take.

FOUR AND TWENTY TAILORS
Went to kill a snail;
The best man among them
Durst not touch her tail.
She put out her horns
Like a little Kyloe cow;
Run, tailors, run,
Or she'll kill you all e'en now.

LITTLE JACK HORNER
Sat in a corner,
Eating a Christmas pie;
He put in his thumb,
And pulled out a plum,
And said, what a good boy am I.

OLD WOMAN, old woman, shall we go a-shearing?
Speak a little louder, sir, I'm very thick of hearing.

Old woman, old woman,
shall we go a-gleaning?
Speak a little louder, sir,
I cannot tell your meaning.

Old woman, old woman,
shall we go a-walking?
Speak a little louder, sir,
or what's the use of talking?

Old woman, old woman,
shall I kiss you dearly?
Thank you, kind sir,
I hear you very clearly.

NOSE, NOSE, jolly red nose,
And what gave thee that jolly red nose?
Nutmeg and ginger, cinnamon and cloves,
That's what gave me this jolly red nose.

HOT CROSS BUNS!
Hot cross buns!
One a penny, two a penny,
Hot cross buns!
If your daughters do not like them
Give them to your sons.
But if you haven't any of these pretty little elves
You cannot do better than eat them yourselves.

JACK BE NIMBLE,
Jack be quick,
Jack jump over
The candlestick.

GEORGIE PORGIE, PUDDING AND PIE,
Kissed the girls and made them cry.
When the boys came out to play,
Georgie Porgie ran away.

LITTLE MISS MUFFET
Sat on a tuffet,
Eating her curds and whey;
Along came a spider
Who sat down beside her
And frightened Miss Muffet away.

BAA, BAA, black sheep,
Have you any wool?
Yes sir, yes sir,
Three bags full:
One for my master,
One for my dame,
One for the little boy
Who lives down the lane.

ONE MISTY, moisty morning,
When cloudy was the weather,
I chanced to meet an old man
Clothed all in leather,
Clothed all in leather
With strap under his chin.
How do you do, and how do you do,
And how do you do again?

MISTRESS MARY, QUITE CONTRARY,
How does your garden grow?
With silver bells, and cockle shells,
And pretty maids all in a row.

This book was set in Goudy Old Style and composed by Characters Typographic Services Inc., New York, New York. Printed by American Printers and Lithographers, Chicago, Illinois and bound by V. Books Press Inc., Brattleboro, Vermont. Separations by Toppan Printing Co. (America) Inc., New York, New York.

Designer: Bruce Zeines
Art Directors: Armand Eisen and Thomas Durwood
Editorial Production: John Woodside
Production: Ellen McNeilly